Parallel Encounters

The Prism's Echo

Book 1

David Scott Fields II

Anchorage, Alaska
www.thrivechristianpress.com

Thrive Christian Press
1120 Huffman Rd. Ste. 24-447
Anchorage, AK 99515

Scripture taken from the New King James Version. Copyright ©
1982 by Thomas Nelson, Inc. Used by permission. All rights
reserved.

First published by Thrive Christian Press on November 24,
2014.

ISBN 978-0-692-32996-2

Published and printed in the United States of America.

This book is dedicated to Jake McNamara and Anthony Walsh, the best Alaska Missions interns I ever had, and two young men I know God is going to use mightily. Thank you both for letting me be a part of your journeys to manhood.

Reader's Note

This mini-series, *Parallel Encounters,* is intended as a spin-off to my *Chronicles of the Imagination* series and will feature some overlap of characters from both universes. This first novella, *The Prism's Echo,* begins a week after Scotty and the Starananians return from Earth's biblical past (as detailed in the novels *Chronicles of the Imagination: Nana-Old Testament* and *Nana-New Testament).* Though the adventure begins on Staranana in the present day, it continues in the far distant future in a universe where history has unfolded far differently than in ours.

Before

"There you are, Dad! I've been looking everywhere for you."

Spikey Moonbeam acknowledged his son with a curt nod, but he did not speak. Why would he? He was totally consumed by what was in his hands. As anyone on Staranana knew by this point, it was not uncommon to find Spikey twisting or turning some gadget he had created in his hands. However, today, barely a week after they had returned from the deep biblical past and the greatest adventure any of them could have possibly imagined, Sparkey Moonbeam saw something much more unusual in his father's hands.

It was a book.

"What are you doing, Dad?" Again nothing but a vague nod, like Spikey somehow knew his son was there, but hardly felt his presence worthy of noting.

"I thought I saw you go in here. Hey, Sparkey, we..." The new voice came from Scotty, the young emperor of Staranana and Sparkey's best friend. The human boy also paused, confused, as Spikey continued to stand with his book, completely ignoring them.

"What is he doing?" Scotty asked.

"Reading," Sparkey replied with a shrug.

"No kidding! This is the library after all!" Scotty quipped and took a slow moment to look around the massive multi-level chamber that was home to more than 1,000,000 unique Starananian literary works. Most were ancient in the extreme – dating almost to the beginning of Emperor Iren's time. In Scotty's brief two-year reign, he had only perused a few of them. Instead, the young emperor had appointed Nicodemus Grass, great grandfather and namesake of the late Nicolas Grass (killed the night Shortstop and his team raided the Palace for supplies), as chief custodian of the library. He was a wizened old bear of 150 years, and he wore thick spectacles positioned halfway down his graying snout. The fact that he could still see at all was something of a miracle, since he had given his younger years over to reading for long hours each night by candlelight. Still, there was no one on Staranana that loved books more than he did (though Garlan was a close second), and giving him the task of cataloguing and restoring the library seemed a fitting task for his twilight years.

Spikey, on the other hand, was not known for frequenting the library. He was not illiterate by any means, but the problem was Spikey's imagination was so acute that any new gadget fictional or fantastic that he might read about in a book, he ended up trying to recreate in real life. This met with varying degrees of success. In fact, rumor had it his *Time Camera*, the invention responsible for their latest foray into the biblical past, had been inspired by *The Time Machine* by H.G. Wells – a book Scotty had lent him. Needless to say, a book in Spikey's hands could be a dangerous thing.

The book in his hands at the moment didn't seem to be a harbinger of doom, but Spikey's friends had learned to play things safe. As with most of the books in the library, it looked as old as the stars themselves. The pages were of a long yellowed parchment, and the cover was made of a soft leather, spotted with holes. The stitch in the binding looked fairly new though, and Scotty and Sparkey both guessed that was part of Nicodemus's restoration campaign. What was most peculiar, however, as Scotty and Sparkey stepped close enough to look over Spikey's shoulders, was the fact that the pages appeared to all be blank. Yet Spikey was turning them as if riveted by some unseen, suspense-filled story.

Scotty grabbed Spikey by the shoulder and began, "Spikey, what are you…"

"AHHHHH!" The inventor screamed and dropped the book to the ground. Miraculously, it did not instantly collapse into dust.

"Spikey, I'm sorry!"

The elder Moonbeam turned to the boy, his heart obviously still pounding in his chest. When he finally caught his breath, he exclaimed, "Now that was an experience!"

"What were you doing, Dad?" Sparkey asked.

"Helping to defend Camelot from the sorceress Morgana le Fay," Spikey said, nonchalantly.

"What?" both boys chimed.

Spikey knelt and picked up the book, which was now closed. Both Sparkey and Scotty could see what appeared to be the title scrawled across the front cover. It was in Starananian script, which Sparkey translated.

"*The Prism's Echo* — What's that, Dad?"

"Something amazing!" Spikey beamed. "Nicodemus showed it to me. How long have I been in here?"

"I don't know; at least a few hours. No one has seen you since lunch," Sparkey said.

"What's so great about that book?" Scotty asked. "From what we could tell, the pages all appeared to be blank."

"*Appeared* is the right word. Here, sit down, boys." They gathered around a small table close by, and Spikey opened the book to what on Earth would have been the title page. On this page, however, there was just one word written in ancient Starananian script.

"*Thimble*," Sparkey translated.

"Thimble?" Scotty questioned.

"Yes, THE Thimble! Do you boys remember General Shortstop and Colonel Speedway telling us about their trip to the snow phoenix city almost two years ago?"

4

"So you think this book was *written* by King Thimble of the snow phoenixes?" Scotty asked.

"Why not? In ancient times, the phoenixes dwelt among the bears just like the angels did."

"But how does a bird write a book?" Sparkey asked.

Spikey scratched his head and replied, "Very carefully, I guess. In any case, according to legend, the phoenixes had powers equal to those of the angels. We already know that they can make *fire glass* and have the ability to hide their city, even though it is unrivaled in size and beauty in all of Staranana."

"So what does that have to do with the book?" Scotty asked.

"Everything! Look, according to some interpreters of the *Text of Iren,* God communicated prophecies about the future to Emperor Iren through the phoenixes. We know that the prophets of the *Bible* were not fortunetellers. The Word of Lord came to them, and they communicated that Word. It was the same for Iren. God communicated His Word through the phoenixes to Iren, and one of those phoenixes, whom I believe to be King Thimble, wrote this book."

"But like Scotty said, the book is blank," Sparkey said.

"That's because it is not meant to be read in the ordinary manner. Call it a book of possibilities. Nicodemus discovered its secrets first, and he showed me. You simply open the book and ask it a question. What happens next is a little difficult to explain."

Here Spikey closed the book and pushed it away from him before continuing. "Do you remember those books about King Arthur and Camelot you brought to the Palace a month or so ago, Scotty?"

"Yes."

"I was reading them before we got sent to the past. I picked up reading them again when we got back. When Nicodemus told me about this book, I asked it, *'What would it be like to visit the realm of King Arthur and Camelot?'* There was a wave of dizziness for a moment, and then I found myself standing in the middle of a vast war camp. There were countless knights there, like I've read about. I even learned some of their names – Gwaine, Lancelot, Perceval – and far too many more to list. They saw me and spoke with me, but they obviously did not see me as a bear, because no one reacted to my appearance. After a time, the memory of my life on Staranana faded away as if it had only been a dream. I joined King Arthur's Knights of the Round Table, and, for more than a year, I joined him on many quests. Just before you brought me back, Morgana le Fay was leading her legions in an assault against Camelot. The last thing I remember is a battle in the throne room and turning to see an arrow shooting toward my chest. That was when I suddenly appeared back here."

"You were never gone, Dad. You were just standing there, mesmerized by that book."

"I know. Unfortunately, I did not follow the one piece of advice Nicodemus gave me – *don't lose yourself in the story.* I believe the book was created to show alternate realities and possibilities. It is not meant to predict the future, but to show what would have happened if history had gone another way. From what I can tell, once a question is posed, it plays out that reality inside the mind of the person who asks."

"That's amazing! But why would Thimble have created such a book in the first place?" Scotty asked.

"Nicodemus has found references to it in a few other places. Apparently, it was given to Iren after he murdered Nana. Ancient theologians believe that it was meant as a way to show Iren what would have happened if he had not killed his son and instead kept his faith in God. From what Nicodemus can tell so far, all mention of *The Prism's Echo* vanishes in books published around 500 years after the death of Nana. It was apparently put in the library and never read again."

"But now we have it!" Scotty smiled.

"Can you ask it anything?" Sparkey asked.

"Apparently not. Nicodemus tried asking it some simple questions about the future like *'What will my wife be serving for dinner?'* But nothing happened. However, when he asked it about alternate possibilities in the past, it responded more than immediately. I think the reason I lost myself in my story is that I was not prepared for what was going to happen. My mind compensated in the only way it could by making me believe I was part of the story."

"But Camelot and King Arthur are legends, not history," Scotty said.

"Even legends can have a basis in history. Still, I don't think that matters. The book seems equally willing to display an alternate fantasy world – even its future. It just won't reveal secrets about the real future."

"I have got to try this!" Scotty squealed and grabbed the book.

"Scotty, no, you can't! We need to…"

The boy opened the book before Spikey could finish his protest and quickly interjected, "We've been studying World War II in school, and I've been wondering what it would have been like if the Nazis had actually taken over the world?"

There was supposed to be more to the boy's query than that. He had a perfectly crafted scenario in his head where he, as a leader in the fight against evil, had mounted a resistance against the Nazis. Two years on Staranana had given him something of a flare for battle strategy. He had not, however, wanted to plunge into a world of darkness forever plagued by that evil regime. Unfortunately, with his question, *The Prism's Echo* began to shimmer with light, and before Spikey or Sparkey could intervene, that is exactly what he got.

Chapter 1
The Ram-Charge Maneuver

"How is Captain Fisher?" asked Lt. Commander Caleb Eli.

First Officer, Commander Lori Brooks felt the captain's bloody neck for a pulse and choked out an answer through tears in a barely audible whisper, "He's dead."

Immediately the pressure was on. With the captain dead, she was in charge, and if she didn't act quickly, they would all soon be joining him. She stood to her feet.

"Eli, take my station. Lt. Commander Smith, what is the status of the SYCO?" she asked, even as the blackened bridge flamed around her. Their vessel, the *Rebel Spaceship Intruder*, was now engaged in a bloody battle with a superior - far superior - Nazi warship. It was like pitting a tin can against a tank, and with half-a-dozen dead crewmembers sprawled all about the deck, it was all she could do but wonder if any of them would get out of this alive.

Smith answered her new captain's question, "Their main power grid is holding, but their hull has suffered some damage along the upper decks. I'd still rather be in their shoes, all things considered."

"It's about time we evened out the odds a bit!"

Brooks turned her eyes toward the helm, only for them to be greeted by the charred and blackened remains of yet another dead crewman – Lt. Walsh, *Intruder's* chief helmsman. Without a capable pilot, her plan was doomed from the start. She began to move to take the station herself, but her eyes hesitated for a moment on a small figure huddled in the corner of the crumbling bridge.

"Commander, more weapons fire is coming in!" shouted Eli.

A few seconds passed, and then the deck bucked, throwing them all across the bridge. Brooks landed next to a blood-soaked body and met the cold, lifeless eyes of a seventeen-year-old ensign. *How many more children would have to die before this madness ended?* She struggled against hot metal and dead, burning flesh to pull herself back to her feet. As she did so, the flash of an exploding bulkhead caught her attention, and again her eyes were on the small figure huddled in the corner. It was another child – the youngest one onboard as a matter of fact – an eleven-year-old acting officer, shaking at one of the sensor stations.

It another time, another place perhaps, the thought of having a child of any age at the heart of this hell would have been unthinkable. But in this time and this place, childhood was a luxury none could afford, so as soon as you were old enough to hold a weapon, you were old enough to fight. Brooks herself had rescued the boy during a brutal Nazi attack back on the lunar colony *New Armstrong*. The boy's parents were dead, and he was alone in universe. The only thing he had left the moon with were the clothes on his back and his name – Scott Fields.

Eli barked, "Commander, the ship is lost! We have to evacuate!"

Her eyes still locked on the panic-stricken young boy, she asked Eli, "Is the propulsion core stable?"

"Yes, but the ship has suffered too much damage. We have to get out of here!" he replied, bracing himself against his panel as another round of missile blasts rocked the ship.

"Not yet!" she protested. Then she turned back to the boy. "Scott, let's make this quick. As acting captain of this vessel, I hereby grant you the field commission rank of lieutenant, and I appoint you chief helmsman. Take your station, Lieutenant."

"Are you crazy?" Eli demanded.

Brooks ignored him.

"Yes, Ma'am!" the boy sounded over the roaring carnage, and even as he moved toward the helm, Brooks could see the fear that previously had him quaking in a corner melting away. She had promoted him for one simple reason. Regulations required an officer with the rank of, at least, lieutenant to man the helm in a time of battle. Despite the fact that the *Intruder's* helmsman was dead, if *Command* learned she had allowed a non-commissioned child to man the helm, she would most likely be stripped of rank when this was over. This was war, and *Rebel Command* would do anything to keep from losing. So they only wanted their best people at their most critical stations. And yet there was something about Scott that Brooks liked. Even at his tender age, he had proven a match for any of *Intruder's* pilots. Nearly a decade of tagging along with his father, one of the best commercial shuttle pilots the moon had ever known, had seen to that. Granted, his promotion wouldn't likely last long – impending death and all hanging over them - but she had full confidence in giving him this chance, despite the stunned and horrified looks certainly forming on the faces of the senior officers standing behind her.

Brooks gave the order to her new helmsman, "Lt. Fields, prepare to initiate the *Ram-charge Maneuver*."

For a moment, a chill ran down Scott's back. Then he replied, "Yes, Commander."

Only Eli protested, "Commander, I understand you not wanting to abandon the ship, but I hardly think a suicide run is a more productive alternative."

"I don't have time for arguments!" commanded Brooks, raising a hand to silence Eli. Then she said, "Commander Smith, bring weapons to full. Target their viewing sphere. It's the most vulnerable part of their ship. Lieutenant Fields, move us to the minimum distance necessary for the maneuver. Commander Eli, put the SYCO on the main holographic viewer."

As Eli complied, a three-dimensional image immediately took shape on a platform in the front of the bridge, along with a series of words. They read, *S.Y.C.O. - Submit, Yield, and Cower to the Omnipotent.* The *Omnipotent* was, of course, what the New Nazi Confederation considered themselves, and the ship on the viewer was sufficient evidence that they were willing to back up the claim.

It was a looming vessel. Seventy meters in length, forty meters wide, with eleven decks fashioned together to form a menacing trapezoid. With seven hundred weapons tubes, it was more than a match for any rebel vessel. In fact, it might have been a match for every rebel vessel combined. Still, Brooks was not willing to let that detour her.

"I'm ready, Commander Brooks," Fields said.

"Acknowledged. Smith, target the viewing sphere, and fire tachyon pulses in one second intervals, on my mark. Scott, lay in a course for the SYCO at maximum sub-light thrust. Prepare to hug their upper hull. We need to get as close as we possibly can to their ship so our weapons will have their full effect. But be careful; we need to come out of this one alive."

Lt. Fields stiffened. He had never found life on the *Intruder* easy, but what was being expected of him now seemed impossible. Brooks saw this and placed a gentle hand on his shoulder. For only an instant, she met the ocean blue eyes of his sandy-haired and soot-blackened head, and in that single glance she did her best to transfer some of her confidence to him. Though, if she was being honest, she didn't have much confidence to spare. She said softly, "Lieutenant, I know you can do this."

That was all he needed. He turned back to his station and said, "At your command."

Smith piped, "Weapons ready, Commander."

"Scott, fire sub-LS thrusters. Smith, confirm target and fire!"

The *Intruder* shot forward in space, racing toward its target like a bullet through the stars. All the while, a pulsing stream of green fire surged from her forward cannons. The pulses ripped through the vacuum, pressing the speed of light. Each pulse left an ugly scorch mark on the hull of the SYCO, but the hull remained uncompromised. The real target, of course, was the viewing sphere.

Though no one quite understood the logic of it, (then again, what logic could an insane empire possibly have), the engineers of the SYCO had shielded their bridge behind nothing but a simple half sphere of glass. Over confidence was the hallmark of Saki Chu's minions. They probably didn't think anyone could get close enough to the viewing sphere to be a threat, and usually they were correct. However, today the *Intruder* was going to prove otherwise.

Another volley of enemy weapons pounded against the hull of the *Intruder*, and Eli asked, "Commander, are you sure this is going to work?"

Brooks said nothing. Instead she dug her fingernails deeply into the arms of her command chair, and she sank her teeth firmly into her already swelling lower lip. If this didn't work, they would all be dead in less than a minute. Thankful that her ebony skin, combined with the near pitch-blackness of the bridge, hid the fears of doom that played across her face, Brooks took a moment to view the features of her crew. At tactical, Leah Smith maintained the poise of a professional. Right beside her, at the secondary command post, Caleb Eli only waited, watching to see if his commander would get them out of this alive. And at the helm, Scott Fields worked frantically. His hands flew from each control on his board, blurring in the dim light. Despite the fact that the maneuvers he was performing required the skills of a veteran, he was performing superbly.

Finally, Brooks's eyes landed on the face of her dead captain. Even despite his lifeless, blood-smeared flesh, his form still demanded the authority his voice had demanded less than ten minutes ago. He had been a paragon of the Christian values and traditions she herself practiced, and, most importantly, he had been her friend – one she could never replace.

Fields counted down the last seconds, "Ten...nine...eight...seven...no damage to the SYCO as of yet...four, three, two...one." And then there was light, followed by a silent blackness.

In space, a vessel flamed into ash. Metal and bones burned, searing and illuminating the night like a super nova, and the agonizing death cries of hundreds of men and women echoed through the void before finally surrendering to their fate. A ship and an entire crew were gone – and it wasn't the *Intruder*. Her thrusters shot her triumphantly through the still enflamed Nazi debris like a phoenix reborn. The rebels had won the day!

On the bridge, Smith, who usually showed no emotion at all, let out the first of countless cheers across the bridge. They had done it! The *Intruder* had destroyed the SYCO in the last second, and even in that short amount of time, Fields had managed to maneuver the ship away from the SYCO, preventing its own annihilation.

Only Brooks and Eli maintained their poise. The new captain called for quiet and addressed them all, "Well done people, but remember we still have a lot of work to do. Commander Eli, you'll assume my former duties as the new first officer. Organize damage control efforts, and get some medics up here to tend to wounded. Have the dead taken to the ship's morgue. We'll all have a lot of grieving to do when we make it back to base. We'll have a brief memorial aboard ship once our repairs are complete."

Brooks's eyes fell on Fisher as she said that, but she quickly turned her attention to Lt. Fields, "Scott, set a course for Jupiter, full sub-LS thrust, and launch a communications probe to relay the results of the battle to our command base on Io."

Finally she said, "I'll be in the chapel if any of you need me." Then leaving her crew to their work, she left the bridge.

~

Several decks below in the sickbay, Dr. Jake Radcliff prepared yet another dead crewman for burial, or rather an icy voyage through the vacuum of space to spend eternity traveling the stars alone in a tiny metal box. This war had begun in the year 2095, and in the 11 years since, he had prepared death certificates for literally thousands. Even the turn of the century had not halted the fighting. Now, six years into the Twenty-second Century, the war was no closer to being over than it had been the day it had begun. Twenty years ago, when he was in medical school, the idea of living from one battle to the next would have seemed ludicrous. He hadn't even considered the military as a possibility. Now, however, the concept of a civilian life was virtually unheard of, and the premature gray in his hair told the haggard story of a war that would certainly claim his and many other lives before too much more time passed. Though it was perhaps a bit of an exaggeration, sometimes he felt like he would gladly sell his soul for a little change of pace.

"First Officer Eli to Dr. Radcliff."

First officer? That was something he'd missed. "Go ahead, sir."

"Please report to the bridge, Doctor. I think we may have something that might interest you."

Radcliff didn't even ask what it was. Word had already reached him that Captain Fisher had been killed. That had been a massive blow. He and the Captain had been friends for a long time, but his adrenaline levels had not quite lowered enough to let him begin grieving. Right now, he would have given anything for an additional distraction that would push thoughts of grief further from his mind. He hoped that whatever bee Eli had in his bonnet would prove up to the challenge.

~

On the bridge, Smith said, "The sensors have been heavily damaged. However, I am certain I can confirm what the probe detected."

"Prepare a full report for the Commander," said Eli.

At that moment, Radcliff stepped onto the bridge and asked, "What is it, sir?"

Eli gestured to Smith who explained, "Our communications probe detected a small metallic object 2,000 kilometers off our port bow. There is one life sign onboard."

"Is it a Nazi escape pod?" he asked.

"No, according to the probe, the object is only about six feet long, and it is composed of minerals that aren't on file. I haven't ruled out the possibility that it is a Nazi device, but I thought you would like to take a look at these readings. The object is emanating a type-one tachyon field."

A grin creased the lines on Radcliff's middle-aged face. "You're right; I would be very interested!" Besides medicine, Radcliff was one of the Rebellion's foremost authorities on *temporal theory*. Though there had been no recorded occurrence of *time travel*, it was theorized that type-one tachyons - different than the type-two variety used as weapons and the type-three variety used for propulsion - could be used to move an object backward or forward through time. Of course, this was all just theory.

"We will reach the object soon. I have already ordered Chief Martinez to attach a grappling cable onto the object once we're in range. Lt. Commander Smith will be standing by with a security team. I want you to examine its passenger," ordered Eli.

"Yes, sir! Gladly, sir!" Radcliff chimed.

~

Brooks breathed softly in quiet meditation. Lit by only a few flickering candles, for this moment, the chapel was her entire universe. Nothing existed but it, herself, and the one true God she loved more than anything. It had been her habit for many years to spend a few hours every evening in quiet communication with God. Though much of the crew shared her beliefs, she found she got far more accomplished when she and God worked one on one. So, never, not even once had she broken her ritual of prayer. Now, however, her meditation was about to be interrupted.

"Commander Brooks, please report to sickbay immediately!" called Radcliff over the intercom.

Brooks opened her eyes in annoyance and asked, "What is it, Doctor?"

"I think the explanation will speak for itself. Please hurry, Commander."

Chapter 2
Double-Double

"What is it, Doctor?" asked Brooks as she entered the sickbay. She still clung to her *Bible*.

"See for yourself, Commander," Radcliff said and gestured across the room.

She turned to see a young boy in a tan jumpsuit sitting on one of the examination tables. At first, she couldn't believe her eyes, and she asked, "Doctor, is this some kind of joke?"

"No, Commander. The young man before you is 100%..." he paused and swallowed hard, "Scott Fields!"

"Emperor Scotty Fields of the planet Staranana, at your service, Commander." The boy sitting on the table smiled broadly and extended his hand to Brooks.

Brooks eyed the hand wearily. As far as she could tell, it was her new helmsman sitting in front of her. She finally shook his hand, but addressed her doctor, still eyeing the boy suspiciously, "Where is Lt. Fields now, Doctor."

Radcliff shook his head in amusement. *Lieutenant Fields? Another new promotion to catalog.* He replied, "On the bridge. Shall I call him, Commander?"

"No, but get a security team down here. In the meantime, run every test you can think of on him. I'll be in the engine room."

"Yes, Commander," he said as she left.

"You'd think she'd have a little more to say to me," the boy chuckled.

"You arrived at a bit of an awkward time. We just survived a battle that cost us the lives of over twenty crewmen, including our captain. Commander Brooks has a bit of a one track mind, and at the moment her ship is her first priority."

"I understand. Being here is a bit of a surprise to me as well."

"Don't worry; we'll get this all straightened out."

"Who is Lt. Fields by the way?"

Radcliff smirked, "I think I'll let the Commander explain that later. Now, let's pull off that shirt and get these tests out of the way."

~

Lt. Commander Leah Smith stood poised over her tactical board, her shoulder length brown hair draped in her face. All of her weapons had been brought back up to peak functional status, and the rest of the repairs were proceeding smoothly. So, for a moment, she glanced about the room, and in seconds her gaze fixed on Commander Caleb Eli. He was smiling at her with a grin that hid no secrets. He liked her, a lot! That much was obvious. The only problem was she didn't care too much for him.

"All tactical systems are back to peak efficiency, sir. Is there anything else I can do for you before I go off duty?" she asked.

"Join me for dinner," he replied, broadening his grin.

"Well I..." she stuttered.

"Lt. Commander Smith, report to the sickbay immediately!" trumpeted Doctor Radcliff's voice over the ship's intercom.

"On my way, Doctor!" she sounded and rushed off the bridge.

Lt. Fields asked, "What was that all about?"

"I don't know!" mumbled Eli, annoyed.

~

"There! The damage to the sub-LS core has been repaired, Commander," reported Chief Engineer Josh Austin. "Fortunately, the damage was minimal."

"Excellent, Chief! Now, how close are we to bringing our new modifications online?" Brooks asked and maneuvered herself toward another circuit panel.

The *Intruder's* engine room was little more than a tiny cubicle containing a crude type-three tachyon fusion engine, capable of reaching speeds one-half that of light. Also included in the bay were ten maintenance tubes, with radiation shielding. These tubes enabled the crew to repair or modify the engine without the risks that came with it. Commander Brooks and Chief Austin were scrunched inside one of those tubes now.

Austin shook his head and replied, "It was a good idea to try it, Commander, but I am beginning to believe light speed travel is a foolish dream. We've been at this for months and barely gotten another 2% efficiency out of the core. I guess humans just weren't meant to travel that fast."

Brooks shrugged off his doubt and quipped, "Ah, come on, Chief, what happened to that *I can do anything* engineer Captain Fisher recruited? I'm not ready to give up. It may take years, but being able to travel at light speed would be a significant tactical advantage over the Nazis."

Austin smirked and turned his attention back to the open relay. He said, "You know, there is always another option."

"You're talking about the Black Vortex Matrix, aren't you? Forget it! That technology is beyond dangerous. It was a mistake for us ever to steal it from the Nazis. I'm just glad Captain Fisher recognized it for what it was."

"You would think traveling faster than the speed of light would be worth a little discomfort. Besides tachyon propulsion is dangerous too."

"You know there is more to it than that, Chief."

Austin nodded. He knew all the superstitions about the technology, though he wasn't quite sure he believed any of them. Black Vortex technology had been available for decades. Long before the Nazis conquered the Earth, there had existed a satanic cult called Rojax. The year was 2020, and the old NASA program had recently sent its first expedition to Mars. During the mission, the space capsule had been struck by a meteor shower while it waited in orbit of Mars. The ship was destroyed, but the astronauts remained safe on the surface. Sending a rescue ship would have taken months, not to mention billions of the old currency called dollars, and the astronauts only had enough provisions to last a few days.

At that point, the leader of the Rojax cult had come forward claiming to have a technology that could rescue the astronauts. It was called a Black Vortex Matrix. The Rojax never explained how it worked, and when the astronauts were returned to earth safe and sound, everyone forgot their questions. What was typically left out of the history books was the fact that each of the astronauts went insane and died of a full cerebral collapse less than a decade later.

When the Nazis took over the planet, they had destroyed what remained of the cult, but not before learning the secrets of the vortex and how to duplicate it. The Black Vortex worked on a principle of collapsing space. The chaotic result could fling a ship or a person up to a full light year in the blink of an eye. However, the effects it had on the human body - ulcers, tumors, and eventual insanity - made it a dangerous combination of science and satanic sorcery. Many believed the technology took a ship straight through Hell itself, and many reported dreams and visions of demons and men and women being tormented in fire after using the technology. Most waved these off as delusions, and since they did not occur in 100% of cases, the BVM was lauded as the next generation of space travel technology. The Nazis used it on a fairly regular basis, but the rebels tended to only use it in extreme emergencies.

Brooks eased the tension of the moment and said, "Besides, Chief, have a little faith. Nothing is impossible for God." And she truly believed that. The Almighty had yet to let her down, and every believing member of the crew could testify to the same. Faith in Christ had proven a far more effective weapon in the fight against the Nazis than any other. Unfortunately, many had also died for that same faith.

Austin nodded and smiled. Then he pointed at a relay and started, "Well, then we will need to..."

"Commander Brooks, please come to sickbay. I have completed my tests." It was Radcliff again.

"He seems to be yelling all over the ship today," Brooks quipped. Then she flipped the intercom switch on the tube wall next to her. "I'll be right there, Doctor."

"What tests?" Austin asked.

"It would take some time to explain, Chief, and frankly, I don't know much myself. Keep working for now. I'll be back as soon as I can."

~

Sickbay was alive with noise when Brooks entered, but no one was in sight. She glanced to her right and found the recovery ward and surgical bay empty. Then she turned her attention to the left and found the science lab to be the source of the noise. Radcliff, the duplicate, and two security guards were there. When the Doctor saw her, he left them and approached her.

"There is no doubt about it, Commander. He is Scott Fields or Scotty as he calls himself. There are no traces of any abnormalities consistent with the cloning process, nor have any surgical alterations been performed on him. As far as I can tell, he is no less Mr. Fields than the one we have sitting on our bridge."

Brooks did not want to ask the next question, but she had no choice. "Then is it possible Lt. Fields is the duplicate. Could the Nazis have captured our Lt. Fields and replaced him with another?"

"Don't you think that's being a little paranoid, Commander? What possible use could an eleven-year-old boy be to the Nazis? Besides, our visitor insists he is from another reality."

"Another reality?"

"I think I'll let him explain."

Brooks nodded and they headed into the science lab. The duplicate Fields was now naked to the waist and hooked up to more than a dozen medical monitors. He certainly looked like the real Fields. He was perhaps a bit more tan, and he didn't have the nasty scars Lt. Fields had on his arms. He also had a more carefree demeanor about him. Like any pre-teen forced into a war, Lt. Fields had long since lost the carefree attitude that typically came with youth. Brooks approached the newcomer and addressed him with suspicion, "What are you doing on my ship?"

"You were the ones who brought me onboard," Scotty retorted.

"Granted. I guess a better question would be - where did you come from?"

Sometime earlier, when Radcliff had asked that same question, a vague thought of an ancient library and a mystic book had flashed through his mind, but something had seized that thought and imprisoned it. Soon that memory was gone, and something that seemed every bit the truth replaced it. Even the evidence of that truth had manifested itself, and the boy accepted it as his own.

"My story may be longer than you have time for, but where I come from it is the early 21st Century."

"So you're from the past?" Brooks questioned.

"Not exactly. You see, about two years ago, I encountered an ancient and alien race called the Starananians. They were being cruelly oppressed by their satanic emperor named Seth. Thanks to the technological genius of my friend, and the chief inventor of Staranana, Spikey Moonbeam, I was brought to Staranana, and I helped the bears defeat Seth."

"Bears?" Brooks questioned, and she looked like she was restraining a laugh.

"It's a long story," Scotty said. Then he continued, "Because of an ancient prophecy and my faith in Jesus Christ, the Starananians made me their new emperor. For the past two years, I have had many adventures with them. On one of those adventures, we encountered a strange vortex in space. For a long time, we thought that vortex was merely a passageway through space. However, a subsequent journey into the vortex ended with my friends and I trapped in Earth's biblical past for more than half a year. When we finally made it home, Spikey wanted to run additional tests on the vortex.

"Eventually, he discovered that the same temporal radiation that sent us into the past, if concentrated in a certain way, could be used to observe alternate timelines…planes of existence where history has unfolded differently."

"I'm familiar with the theory," Brooks said.

"Well, Spikey managed to lock in on one alternate timeline – yours I suppose – but after what happened to us during the whole *Bible* times adventure, he didn't want to risk taking a ship in too close to investigate. Instead, he built what he called an interdimensional pod, a probe of sorts that could observe the parallel universe phenomenon at close range without putting an actual person in danger."

"Fascinating!" Radcliff interjected, though the look on Brooks's face indicated that she was less than convinced.

Scotty continued, "Spikey launched his pod from the surface of Staranana, but just before it entered the vortex, its autopilot malfunctioned. There was no ship in range to retrieve the pod before it entered the vortex, so Spikey decided to use the *Door*."

"Door?" Brooks questioned.

"A transportation device that sends a person instantly from one place to another. Spikey had the foresight to equip the pod with enough space to accommodate a single passenger once manned missions were deemed safe. Spikey decided to send in someone to check on the pod. It was to a be quick two minute mission to activate the manual piloting systems and turn the probe away from the vortex until it reached a safe position where it could be retrieved and repaired. The only problem was, with the pod already sealed, the only person small enough to materialize inside without hurting himself was…me. Spikey wasn't going to let me go, but eventually I prevailed upon him. He sent me aboard, and I started my mission. However, I was barely aboard the pod for a minute before I felt a sharp jolt. I must have lost consciousness after that because that next thing I remember was waking up in your sickbay."

"The vortex must have dragged your pod in and sent you through the dimensional barrier," Radcliff hypothesized.

Scotty nodded in agreement, but Brooks said, "That is an unusual explanation. I'm not quite ready to except it. There is still the possibility that you are some sort of Nazi deception. For the time being, you will be confined to this sickbay. I will contact Io and see if they have any information about you."

"Wait! Did you say *Nazi*?" Scotty asked.

"That also is a long story. Unfortunately, I don't have time to tell it right now."

Brooks turned to leave, but the new Scotty got up, half pulling the equipment he was attached to off their counters. "Commander, please, if I may, I have records and other technologies in my pod that can prove I am who I say I am. I'd even be willing to share my technology with you if it can help in your struggle. Just give me a chance to prove myself."

Brooks gave the visiting Scotty a quizzical look, but then Dr. Radcliff interrupted, "Commander, if you'll allow Lt. Fields to come down here, I'll run a few more tests. Perhaps, if I examine a fresh sample of each of their DNA, I can learn a bit more."

"I heard you mention him before. Who are you talking about?" Scotty asked.

Brooks smiled. It was her turn to offer this kid a bit of a shock. "It appears, *Your Highness*, that you are in for a surprise yourself. You see, Lt. Scott Fields, a young man who looks very much like you, is an officer aboard my ship."

"Oh, so that's why you guys are making such a big deal about me. I've been through some intense medical examinations before, but nothing like this – and if you knew how meticulous my doctor friend Gloria is, you'd know that is saying a lot. Even so, your Lt. Fields won't be the first duplicate of myself I've encountered. I'd love to meet him."

Brooks nodded and turned back to the Doctor, "I'll send Lt. Fields down. Let me know when your tests are finished." Radcliff acknowledged her as she left, even as he pushed Scotty back toward the examination table.

~

An hour or two passed as Brooks waited anxiously on the bridge. Manning the helm herself, since Fields was absent, she could not help but feel uneasy about the newcomer. He was like something out of science fiction. It was true that over the years science had made many advancements similar to those predicted by science fiction, but most of those were in the hands of the Nazis. Mostly the rebels had to scrounge for anything they might need. The technology the new Fields had described seemed almost inconceivable, and the very fact that he was a *new* Fields was enough to set anyone on edge. Brooks had always believed young Scott to be special. Why else would she have given him the helm at the mere age of 11? Still, the idea that God for some reason had created an alternate universe where an alternate version of this boy not only existed but was emperor of a vast planet seemed ludicrous at best. Would they find out there were alternate versions of all of them out there somewhere? For that matter, would they find out there were alternate versions of the God she loved so much?

That she would not accept. No matter what universe it was written in, the *Bible* was clear. The Lord had said of Himself in Isaiah 43:10-11, **"Before Me there was no God formed, nor shall there be after Me. I, even I, am the Lord, and besides Me there is no savior."** That felt pretty all inclusive to her – alternate realities notwithstanding. No, there had to be more to this than what the duplicate had said.

~

It seemed an eternity before Radcliff finally called her back to the sickbay. Now both Fields's were lying on examination tables, bare-chested and hooked up to more medical devices than she cared to count. Lt. Fields looked a little uncomfortable and cold. He didn't seem too enthused with meeting his counterpart either. The traveler, on the other hand, seemed excited and intrigued at the opportunity to meet his double.

Brooks gave her attention to Radcliff as he reported, "I did find one significant difference between these two, Commander."

"What is it?"

Radcliff opened his mouth for an instant, but he did not speak. He had been about to spout off something about temporal lobes and neural membranes, but he figured he'd get nothing but blank stares for his trouble, so he cut to the chase.

"They're brains are vastly different, Commander. They may be genetically identical, and it is more than possible that they came from alternate versions of the same parents, but their minds have been influenced by events in two different time periods – creating two distinct personalities. They may share the same DNA and appearance, but the similarities end there."

"A little confusing but accurate," piped Scotty.

"Tell me something - Scotty…" Lt. Fields found it just a tad on the weird side to be addressing himself, "…are the Nazis in control of your world?"

"No. Why?" replied Scotty.

"It makes sense. Even in our timeline, the Nazi weren't around in the early 21st Century," noted Radcliff.

"Granted, but if he is from an alternate reality, shouldn't he at least be from the same time period as us? He did tell us he was from almost 100 years in the past," Brooks questioned.

"Who can say, Commander? Perhaps time flows differently in different realities. Perhaps somewhere out there we're all pioneers on the American prairie," Radcliff chuckled.

Brooks didn't even attempt to hide her smirk at that, but said, "Regardless, we've established the fact that our two universes are very different, and that, for the moment, there is sufficient evidence to believe our guest is who he says he is. Now the question becomes what do we do about it?"

There was a long pause as heads were scratched and chins rubbed raw. Then Lt. Fields snapped his fingers and excitedly offered an idea. "I know! Maybe we can find a way to transport all the rebels to his universe. It sounds a whole lot better than ours."

Lt. Fields's fellow crewmembers seemed enthused by the idea, but then Scotty barked, "No! You can't! I've heard enough of Spikey's tech talk to guess that moving an entire civilization from one universe to the next would have a devastating effect on time and space. Besides, your people wouldn't fit in on Staranana, and my Earth is from almost 100 years in the past compared to yours."

"Well, then why are you here anyway?" demanded Fields. He had never felt so disgusted looking at his own face before. Without the Doctor's permission, he pulled the medical monitors off his body, grabbed his shirt, and headed for the door.

"As you were, Lieutenant!" Brooks snapped. Though the age of 11 and tantrums sometimes went hand in hand, as an officer now, Fields should have known better. Then again, meeting one's doppelganger was, perhaps, excuse enough for a tiny tantrum.

The boy halted in his tracks next to the sickbay exit and snapped to attention – his shirt only halfway pulled back on. Brooks walked to him, took him by the shoulders and said, "You know we can't abandon the people back on Earth, and you also know God works all things out for the good. This may be a little awkward for you, but I need you to put that aside. Consider that an order, Lieutenant."

Fields nodded reluctantly, and she said, "The Doctor and I can finish up here. Why don't you return to your post?"

Fields exhaled; his anger ebbing. Then he nodded and left the room. When he was gone, Scotty addressed the Commander, "Ma'am, I don't know much about your struggle, but since I'm here, I would like to help."

"Thank you, but how much can one eleven-year-old hope to accomplish?" she asked.

"A great deal, judging by my counterpart, ill-tempered as he is. Commander, I know there is something I can do. What is the harm in letting me try? Just give me a few hours and a computer. I'll see what I can come up with," assured Scotty.

"Very well, but we will have to arrange some form of compensation. I am not quite sure what we could offer you."

"I could use some help repairing my pod, and I need energy. I have a theory that if I can send a strong enough signal back through the vortex, Spikey will be able to use the *Door* to get me home. The vortex has openings in hundreds of star systems. If your universe is like mine, there should be a microscopic event horizon orbiting the moon. I just need to get in range."

"I'll see what I can work out. In the meantime, I will assign you a bunk in the crew quarters. Then I will have one of my officers escort you to the records department. You will find plenty of computers there."

"Thank you, Commander," Scotty said. Then he turned to Radcliff and asked, "Can I put my shirt back on now? You do keep it kind of chilly in here."

Radcliff smirked, and began removing his medical monitors. This was sure to be an interesting mission.

Chapter 3
History

"You should find what you need in here, sir," said the young ensign who had led Scotty into the *Intruder's* records center. If Scotty could compare it to anything, it looked like the computer lab in his school, though his computer lab wasn't nestled in a battleship currently hanging in deep space. The officer logged in to one of the terminals and then gestured that Scotty should sit down. He said, "This icon here that looks like a book will allow you access to our non-classified records."

Scotty smirked. Despite the fact that this ship was supposed to be from the 22nd Century, these computers looked like they had come from the 1990s. The young officer turned to leave, but Scotty halted him, "Wait! Ensign...?"

"Tanner Michaels, sir."

"Nice to meet you, Ensign Michaels. I was wondering...well...Commander Brooks said that your Earth is in the control of the Nazis. She didn't have time to tell me how that happened, but I was wondering if you might have the time to tell me?"

Michaels smiled and said, "Actually, I was just going off duty, and I'd be happy to tell you."

He took a seat beside the boy and pondered, "Oh, where to begin? I suppose I should start centuries ago, long before the war. In fact, it starts at the end of another war called *World War II*."

"We had one of those too," Scotty said.

"Yes, well, it was the end of a very difficult era in human history. The inevitable fall of the German Empire and the Nazi reign of terror had finally come to pass. Adolf Hitler, mad man and former dictator of Germany, had escaped death at the hands of his enemies by killing himself. Many thought this was the end of his evil, but they were very wrong.

"A man by the name of Colonel Saki Chu, a ruthless and charismatic Japanese officer, tied to the Nazis only through his German mother, refused to accept defeat. The destruction of his hometown Nagasaki and the deaths of his entire family in 1945 after the American atomic attack only strengthened his resolve. He fled to the Middle East and began plans for the rise of the second Nazi regime."

"I've spent some time in the Middle East of my Earth recently. What happened to the Jews in your universe?" Scotty asked.

Millions upon millions died. Hitler seemed intent on exterminating every last one of them, and untold numbers met gruesome ends in his concentration camps. When the war ended and the camps were librated, no one could have guessed the miraculous set of circumstances that would occur in the next three years. By 1948, the Jews had been reestablished in their ancestral lands, and the nation of Israel was reborn – after millennia of nonexistence."

"I'm betting Colonel Chu wasn't too happy about that."

"No, he wasn't, and hiding in the heart of what used to be called Iraq, he was certain he would find the hatred he needed to kindle the Nazi flame anew. However, the world was changing, and soon the name Nazi became synonymous with Satan. Even those nations that had long hated the Jews and might have joined Hitler given the chance feared retaliation from the victors of the war. No one seemed willing to join Chu on his tirade.

"For the next few decades, the Colonel traveled the world, gathering supporters wherever he could. However, by the late 1970s, an aging Saki Chu was growing weary of his travels, none of which had been very successful.

"Of course, the Colonel didn't see what was so horrible about the Nazi philosophy. To him, the idea of weeding out the inferior members of the human race, both physically and mentally, could only benefit the species. Unfortunately, the rest of the human race didn't quite see things that way. By Chu's way of thinking, they lacked a sense of greatness, and that in itself made him think them inferior; but at his age there was becoming little he could do to fight the ignorance and simplicity of the world. At least, that is what he thought."

"Let me guess; he suddenly had a streak of luck that put him back on top and made him ruler of the entire world," Scotty interjected sarcastically.

"Who's telling this story you or me?" Michaels chuckled. "Now, like I was saying, Saki was about to get the break of a lifetime! In Germany, somewhere just north of Berlin I think, there existed a small, rundown research college. No student worth two cents would go near the place, but a certain group of individuals did find the location of a particular value. The college possessed a highly experimental cryogenics laboratory."

"You mean like suspended animation? I spent about a week in a device like that recently. You see, I…oh, well, that story can wait."

"I assume the procedures were similar. The tall and short of it is that the lab froze people so they wouldn't die. The people would then be thawed at a later date. Mostly it was used for people who were terminally ill, in the hope that a treatment for their disease would be found in the future, and they could be revived. It was quite the craze in the late 20th Century. Rumor has it that Walt Disney, the famous cartoonist, was frozen. I never heard if they ever revived him."

"I guess Disneyland made it to all universes," Scotty chuckled. "Though in my universe the whole Disney being frozen thing was just an urban legend with no truth to it."

Michaels shrugged and then continued, "Seeing no other alternative, Saki had himself frozen. It was the Colonel's hope that at some later date, the hatred people had for Nazis would not be quite so intense, and their empire could rise once more. And so he slept, for over one hundred years, never to awaken until the year 2095."

"Can I ask a question?" Scotty asked.

"Certainly."

"Well, how did Saki get enough Nazis to take over the solar system? You can't do much recruiting when you've been frozen for a century."

"That's the next part of the story. You see, no one spends decades wandering the world looking for recruits without a whole lot of money in the bank. Chu's grandfather had been the CEO of a highly successful multinational corporation. He had died before the war, and though most of the infrastructure of his corporation was destroyed during the atomic attacks, he had set up a trust for Saki in a Swiss bank before his passing. No one knows exactly how much was put into the trust, but rumor had it the interest alone was worth millions each year – and that is saying a lot for such an economically depressed era. Saki left behind that fortune, which was submitted to what remained of the Nazi party. They were assigned to use the money to build an army to take on the world. Saki wanted ships, fighter planes, troops, and weapons. There had to be enough to take on even the greatest military forces. The leaders of the Nazis were also assigned to seize power if the opportunity presented itself, but it never did. And so for generations the Nazis trained their youth so that they would all be prepared for the glorious return of their master."

"Why didn't they all just run off with the money?" Scotty asked.

"I suppose it is because the recruits Chu was able to gather thought of him as something of a god. He had every bit of Hitler's charisma, if not more. And, of course, there were the miracles."

"Miracles?"

"Rumors only; no hard evidence was ever found. However, the Nazis alive today still tell stories of Chu's abilities to heal the sick and raise the dead. I suppose the recruits living back then would have done anything for him, and I am sure many hoped and prayed every day that they would live long enough to see his glorious return. If you ask me though, his return was anything but glorious."

"What do you mean?"

"Here, let me show you," Michaels said. He scooted in closer to Scotty's computer and clicked the book icon. After typing in some search parameters, several paragraphs of text appeared on the screen. The Ensign continued, "Our databanks contain literally thousands of journals and letters from people who were involved in the early days of the war on both sides. This is a copy of a letter written by the man who revived Saki Chu."

Scotty leaned in closer to the computer and began to read:

'Mother,

I couldn't believe my eyes. He was so menacing and deadly. Even standing there, naked, exposed to the world, as he was, I would not have dared to challenge him. He was like a beast of legend - a demon risen from Hell itself! Oh, I'm sorry; I should tell you what I'm talking about.

This morning, September 11, 2095, the colonel woke up. That's right; the long awaited return of Saki Chu has finally come. I was the officer on duty when time ran out, and his cryogenics chamber deactivated. It was a sight I tell you, and was I ever scared. However, I had my orders.

Saki awoke disoriented and quite literally mindless. We had expected this though and had readied some equipment to - let's just say - reboot the Colonel. We also pumped him full of chemicals to stimulate his heart and cell replication process. Forgive me for using these technical terms, Mother. It's just easier for me.

It took us some time to calm him down and begin the procedure. I brought a few more men in to help me restrain him. However, after about three hours of work, the Colonel was dressed, awake, and in his right mind. And his body was now as healthy and fit as a twenty-year-old, thanks to our efforts.

His first question was, "What of my empire?"

I'd have answered him right then, but you see, he had his hands around my throat. So all I could do was point out the window to the balcony. Saki stepped out onto the balcony. Below he saw it, and he just started laughing. I have to go for now mother. I will write again soon.

Your son,

Thomas'"

"That's a rather abrupt letter!" Scotty sneered. "What did he see?"

"No one is quite sure. Some think it was a small portion of his army. Others think it was his flagship, the *Berserko*. No one quite agrees, but whatever it was, it spelled the deaths of over half the human population. Saki led his forces through the Earth waging war. Those governments whom he could not overthrow fell to spies he planted to betray their secrets to him. And as if his brute force was not enough, Saki developed another weapon to use against his enemies.

"They were called simply the B.O.Ts. A race, or races rather, of half-machine, half-animal genetic hybrids. It was a regular Doctor Frankenstein project. The beasts were brutal and heartless. Well, all but one that is, but you can hear more about him later. Sufficed to say, Saki conquered Earth in less than three years. By the dawn of the 22nd Century, there was no further resistance on Earth – just devoted servants and worshippers and several nations' worth of crippled and maimed slaves – save one that is."

"Which one?"

"You can probably guess. Almost no rebel has been back to Earth since the war began, but there are stories – and I pray they are more than rumors – that Saki Chu never invaded Israel."

"Why not? It was the Jews Hitler hated in the first place."

"Who can say? Most of the stories say the Jews are hold up within their own borders, waiting for an imminent attack, but if the stories are right, none has ever come. If you ask me, Chu is trying to turn Israel into the largest concentration camp in history. It has been 11 years since any other nation has traded with them. They should be running out of resources, but all the stories say their land is flourishing, and the Jews think this is the last great conflict before their Messiah comes."

"You mean the Great Tribulation?"

"The what?"

"From the book of *Revelation*…"

"Huh?"

"You read the *Bible* don't you?"

"Sure, but I've never heard of a book of *Revelation*."

"Interesting. Maybe that's something I can share later, but go on with your story. The Jews aren't fighting, nor is anyone else on Earth, but obviously some sort of rebellion still exists."

"Earth established its first extra-planetary colonies in the early 2070's. Mars and the Earth's moon were first. There were also outposts set up in the asteroid belt and on the moons of Jupiter – the most prominent being on Io. Space propulsion technology was still rather crude and expensive in those days, so once they were established, the colonies were fairly self-governing. In fact, by the time most of the colonists had even heard about the war, it was too late to do anything about it. Soon enough, the Nazis cut off the trade lanes back to Earth, and over three million people were left to fend for themselves without the possibility of ever going back home.

"It wasn't long before Chu set his sights on the extra-planetary colonies. When they realized war was coming their way, the colonist converted what cargo and transport ships they had into warships. The *Intruder* itself used to be an asteroid mining vessel named the *Breakaway*. It was rechristened three years ago when it was the first rebel vessel to break through Nazi lines and rescue three rebel officials who had been taken hostage. That mission earned Captain Fisher his command. The original skipper of the *Breakaway* was killed during that mission, and now that Fisher is dead, I guess Brooks will be our new captain."

Scotty nodded and asked, "So what happened with the colonists?"

At first, we had a hundred ships between all the colonies, but when the Nazis came, they came in force. In the year 2101, the SYCO fleet wiped out the colony on Mars. Last year, after a bloody standoff that lasted months, the colony on the moon was destroyed. That was where your counterpart lived. Brooks and a small team from the *Intruder* were able to evacuate about 100 of the 80,000 colonists. Lt. Fields was one of them. The rest of the colonist were either killed in the fight, or captured by Chu. We later learned he had more than 40,000 civilians ejected naked into the vacuum of space. Occasionally one of our ships will run across one of their corpses floating like debris in the void. It is not a pretty sight."

Scotty's stomach churned, and he asked, "What happened to the rest of colonies?"

"Of the three million original colonists, only about 50,000 were left alive by the end of 2105 – last year. The non-combatants reside primarily in the asteroid belt. The colonies there are all subterranean, and the belt is too dense for Nazi vessels to maneuver. For the most part, those colonies have been left undisturbed.

"The ten thousand or so who wanted to fight formed a rough military coalition called *Rebel Command*. Everyone on this ship serves in *Rebel Command*. We took over the colonies in the moons of Jupiter and converted them completely for military purposes. From there, we continue a fight that has lasted over a decade – and seems no closer to its conclusion."

"Maybe I can help with that," Scotty said, and for half a second, the confidence the boy radiated flared up a spark of hope in Michaels he thought long since extinguished.

"Maybe you can," the ensign said with a sober nod. Then he smiled and said, "I'll leave you to your work."

Chapter 4
The Plan

On the bridge, Lt. Fields sat drumming his fingers against his piloting controls. At the moment, the *Intruder* was hanging motionless in space, and though there was plenty of work to be done repairing damaged systems, the helm was not one of them, and this *Fields* was no technician. Physically speaking, he wasn't really even strong enough to help move the debris or dead bodies from the bridge. Though he hadn't sensed it yet, he worried that the crew would ultimately come to resent his promotion, or worse that Commander Brooks would rescind it now that the crisis was over. Even though it had been less than a day since he was commissioned, he liked having a useful role to play on the ship. Even so, for the moment, there was nothing he could do but watch his comrades working, and that left him feeling a little bored.

However, it was barely a moment later that the whining hiss of the elevator door absolved his boredom as it deposited someone new onto the bridge. At first, only Fields saw the newcomer, but then Eli did. Brooks had briefed her crew on the traveler, but there was no hiding the shock on Eli's face. He nodded toward the upper level, and Commander Brooks turned her attention toward the elevator.

Brooks stood up and said, "Ah, Mister Fields, let's have that report you promised me."

The Commander had managed to get over the initial shock she had felt at meeting the new Scotty. Her crew, with perhaps the exceptions of Dr. Radcliff and Lt. Fields, hadn't had that luxury. Commander Smith instinctively moved her hand closer to her sidearm (though she had already seen the boy). Commander Eli followed Brooks to the upper level as if guarding her, and the rest of the bridge crew just stared at the duplicate. Many were even looking constantly back and forth between the two Fields's searching for some distinguishable difference between them.

Emperor Scotty smiled as he handed Brooks a tablet. "Commander, I have discovered a major Nazi weakness. If you will call your senior staff together, I will explain it in more detail."

A few minutes later, Brooks and her senior officers sat around an oval conference table in the galley. On the left sat Leah Smith. Next to her sat Chief Engineer Josh Austin. Of Canadian descent, he was stalky but muscular with black hair and big green eyes. He was perhaps not the best engineer the rebellion had to offer, but one thing was certain; he never did less than his best on anything. One afternoon with him when they first met had proved to Brooks that he brought an enthusiasm to his job that few more experienced engineers shared. On her recommendation, Fisher had appointed Austin his chief engineer.

Again on the left was Chief of Transportation Klaus Martinez, a native of Mexico. He and his family had moved to the asteroid colonies in 2094. He was only ten at the time, and now at 22 he was still young and conservative, yet playful. As a pilot, he was perhaps more qualified to take over the helm than Lt. Fields, but he would be the first to admit he preferred piloting smaller craft. He ran the launch bay and its crew like clockwork, and whenever *Command* had a new vehicle to test, he was the pilot they came to. It was a far more exciting job than being a mere helmsman. He had often teased Lt. Commander Walsh about that, and without doubt, Lt. Fields would soon come under his torment as well.

Finally on the left was the strangest crewmember of all. If Scotty hadn't spent so much time around strange and frightening creatures on Staranana, he might have refused to enter the room when he saw Agent Loso. What was unique about Loso was the fact that he was not human. He was a B.O.T., the only one in the rebellion. He had been one of the very first B.O.Ts. (Bionic Organism Technology) the Nazis had ever created, and being a prototype he had many problems. His main problem was in his loyalty chip. When he was serving the Nazis, he was deemed unreliable and untrustworthy. The Nazis had attempted reprogramming him seventeen times before deciding to terminate him.

When the rebellion learned about Loso, they realized the potential a rebel B.O.T. would have. They sent an engineer/spy to see if they could make heads or tails of this malcontented droid. It turned out they could. They replaced his loyalty chip and programmed him to be a rebel spy. After faking his death, he assumed a new identity and infiltrated the Nazi for three years. After that, he was assigned to the *Intruder* so the rebels could put his knowledge and the strength of his cybernetic reptilian body to good use. To be perfectly honest, Loso reminded Scotty of another cybernetically enhanced reptile he had recently encountered.

Brooks at one end of the table gestured to Scotty at the other. Who then in turn addressed Fields, Eli and Radcliff on the right, as well as those on the left. As he tapped a few controls, the holographic image of a huge space station suddenly formed above the table. It had a large round top, and from there it extended downward in a stair-step series of smaller round sections.

Scotty reported, "This is the Nazi Space Port. It has the weapons and resources to take on more than double the fleet it serves. It also controls a network of satellites that form a spherical energy barrier that completely encompasses the Earth. No ship can enter or leave the planet's atmosphere as long as that grid is activated."

"We already know about all this! What does it have to do with any of us?" questioned Lt. Fields in annoyance.

"Just about everything!" returned Scotty, meeting his double's gaze with determination. "Since the early days of computer technology, computer operators have taken extreme caution in protecting their systems from magnetic disturbances. Despite all the advancements science has made since the early days, computers can still be disrupted by magnetic fields. The Space Port's computers are no exception. I have a theory of how we can use this fact to our advantage. My pod has the ability to emit a large, highly disruptive magnetic field.

It is part of what helps it scan beyond a dimensional barrier. So if we could..."

"So if we can get your pod aboard the Space Port and engage the field, we can disable the station. An assault launched at the precise moment the station deactivates will enable the rebels to destroy the station and open access back to Earth," piped Martinez.

"Or..." Brooks began, "...we can commandeer the station for ourselves and keep the bulk of the Nazi fleet bottled up on the Earth for years. The station's defenses could easily put down any resistance from any SYCO vessels that might still be patrolling the solar system."

"My thought exactly, Commander. Once the station's defenses go down, the Nazis can quickly and easily be driven out," responded Scotty.

"The question remains, how do we get the pod onboard?" asked Eli.

"One thing you must keep in mind is the fact that I need to be in the pod when it is activated. Tuned correctly, the magnetic field should be enough to penetrate the barrier back into my reality. If I know my friend Spikey, he's got the *Door* all set to bring me home the instant he makes contact with me. If he locks onto the pod without me, I will be stranded here, and I'm guessing God never meant for two Scotty Fields's to be running around this universe."

"All that noted for the moment, how do we get the pod onboard?" asked Brooks, repeating Eli's question.

"Commander, I may have just the thing," piped Martinez. Rising, he related with excitement, "For the past few months, I have been working to reconfigure a transport space jet to Nazi specifications. Make the pod look like a piece of space cargo, and it will be simple to get it aboard. We can use the *TSJ* to trick the Nazis into letting us come aboard freely, and if Loso pilots the craft, it will be all the more convincing."

"Very well. Loso, you will take the *TSJ* in. The rest of you get ready. We will proceed with the plan first thing tomorrow," ordered Brooks, shuffling her crew to their duties. Only Lt. Fields remained in his seat.

Commander Brooks addressed him, "That means you too, Lieutenant."

Fields rose, and with his skepticism plainly obvious on his face, he said, "Yes, Commander!" Then he left the room.

Chapter 5
The Space Port

"Space Port, this is B.O.T unit 77703.9, requesting docking clearance, over," the words belonged to Loso. He was now in the reconfigured *TSJ*, and Scotty's pod was magnetized to the ship's belly. It was disguised as a medical cargo container to avoid suspicion. In a few moments, it would be time to put their scheme into play.

Transport Space Jets, commonly referred to as *TSJs*, were the rebellion's main form of short range transporters. Each wing could pivot or fold into a variety of positions, making the jets ideal for squeezing through close quarters. The cockpit, being small, could seat only two people comfortably. The pilot sat in front, and the tactical officer sat in the back. Their ability to travel at nearly $1/1000^{th}$ light speed (or about 300 kilometers per second) and excellent maneuverability made them ideal for short range missions in space.

"Confirmed, you are cleared to dock in bay twenty-three," replied a docking master over the outer space transmitter.

"Acknowledged," replied Loso. At that moment, every professional part of Loso was ready for the mission at hand. Personally though, he was terrified, and he found his mechanical arms trembling. Fear of their Nazi masters had been a key component in the programming of all B.O.Ts. His reprogramming had tempered that fear. Even so, when he was a spy, he had always feared being found out. That was impossible, of course, due to the fact that he was virtually identical to all the other reptile B.O.Ts. the Nazis possessed. Despite this reassurance, he couldn't help feeling edgy when dealing with the Nazi.

~

*"**Commander Lori Brooks reporting: Earth date 3-23-2106.** I have sent Agent Loso and the counterpart Fields on a seemingly impossible mission. It is the belief of our guest that a highly disruptive magnetic field, which he has the means to produce, can render the Nazi Space Port powerless. At this moment, the two previously mentioned gentlemen are carrying out this mission. They sneaked aboard by means of a reconfigured TSJ, set to Nazi specifications. The Intruder is currently in hiding above the dark side of the moon. In six hours, we will move into the light. If everything goes according to plan, by the time we emerge, Scotty's task will be complete. With little effort on our part, we can seize control of the station. However, we are requesting backup just in case. You will find a full report of our plans in our logs. Brooks out!* **Second Code:** *May God bless this mission!"*

~

"Log probe dispatched, Commander," reported Smith.

"Very good, Ms. Smith," replied Brooks. Then she turned to her Scott, "Lt. Fields, when will the probe reach our base on Io?"

"Barring any problems, it will reach Io in one hour," responded Fields as he punched up the information on his board.

"That gives them five hours to respond. I hope Loso and Scotty are ready."

~

"Stand aside, Unit! I am under orders to inspect your cargo!" demanded an agitated human in a Nazi lieutenant's uniform.

"There are highly perishable medical supplies in that hold. I am under superior orders to get these supplies through customs quickly and down to the planet. I am also under orders to keep the container sealed at all times. So I cannot allow you access to my cargo!" protested Loso, bearing his synthetic B.O.T. teeth.

"MOVE ASIDE! You cannot have orders superior to those given to me directly from Emperor Saki Chu," ordered the Nazi lieutenant, removing his weapon and directing the barrel at Loso.

Loso swallowed hard. If Chu was onboard the station, then their mission had just gone from seemingly impossible to definitely impossible. Loso's mechanical mind had only facts, no superstitions. Even the Christian faith so many of the rebels clung to was difficult for him to grasp. Still, if the reports could be believed, Chu boasted supernatural powers of demonic proportion. It was said that no one could lie to him, for as a master of lies himself, he could see through any one of them. To be sure, there was no more deadly threat than the sinister Nazi leader.

"Very well," surrendered Loso. The B.O.T. led the way to the container, but he had no intentions of opening it.

There was a stutter in his clipped mechanical voice as he said, "The access code is rather complicated. It will take a few moments to enter it."

"Just get on with it!"

"Lieutenant, we need you over here for a moment!" came a voice from across the bay.

The lieutenant cursed under his breath and then said, "Don't go anywhere! I will be right back!"

Loso felt every ounce the coward planning what he was about to do, but the success of this mission hinged on at least one of them remaining free. At the moment, things were not looking the best for the counterpart Fields, but if he could escape, there was still a chance the mission could be accomplished. When the lieutenant's back was finally turned, he did the only thing he could; he stood and walked slowly into a crowd of B.O.Ts. working on the opposite side of the bay. He soon slipped through their numbers and into a corridor. He was home free. Scotty, on the other hand, wasn't so fortunate.

~

"Where is he going?" Scotty cursed as he watched the tiny blip on his pod's viewing screen that represented Loso's life signs slowly move away from him and then disappear. The screen and the assurance of Loso's presence (however much he looked like the *Viper* not withstanding) were about the only things keeping Scotty from a severe claustrophobic attack. If and when he ever returned to Staranana, he had plans to make any device like this shiny space coffin illegal. Spikey himself might just have to face some jail time for building the accursed thing!

The screen lit up with more life signs – about four humans judging by the readouts, and after a moment, Scotty could hear their muffled voices outside the pod.

"Where did that B.O.T. go?"

"Who cares? Those things have always have given me the creeps anyway. Just get that container open, and let's get this inspection over with."

"The B.O.T. said there was a code."

Scotty let out a sigh of relief. Spikey had never said anything about there being a code, but it also wasn't like him to leave his inventions unsecure. If there was a code, they'd never get inside. Then again, the crew of the *Intruder* had somehow gotten him out earlier. This was not good!

"Let me take a crack at it, Lieutenant," came one of the voices. Almost immediately, one of the human blips moved closer to the pod and his voice became much clearer. Scotty heard him begin to tap on the outside control panel of the pod. After several minutes, he stopped, and Scotty heard him say, *"It's heavily encrypted. It might take several hours to breach, but take a look at this, sir."*

Another blip drew closer and Scotty heard the voice of the lieutenant ask, *"What is it?"*

"My hand scanner is detecting life support equipment inside of this cargo container."

"It is supposed to be medical equipment. Maybe there are biological samples."

"Maybe, but that doesn't explain these life sign readings. I think there is a person in there."

Scotty could practically hear the grin crossing the lieutenant's face. *"Oh, I have to see this, someone is trying to sneak a person through customs. Are you sure we can't get it open?"*

"Not for a while, sir."

"Then let's take it down to the incinerator."

"That probably won't damage the pod, sir."

"No, but I have a feeling the excess heat will give whoever is hiding inside there second thoughts about coming out. Here, maybe the four of us can manage it."

Scotty felt the pod shake as the four Nazis hoisted it into the air. Spikey hadn't said anything about the pod being heat resistant, but he supposed if it could travel between universes, it must be somewhat heat resistant. Still, could he take that chance? Or should he proceed with the plan now? Spikey would no doubt be watching, and a *Door* field could bring him home at any time. The rebels had repaired his pod, and he had enough power to activate the magnetic field, but the *Intruder* wouldn't be ready yet. Loso hadn't struck him as a coward or a traitor, so he must have had a good reason for leaving, and Scotty had certainly been in worse scrapes than this. He decided it was it was time for an extraordinary leap of faith.

~

"It's a bit heavier than it looks," winced one of the four Nazis.

"Quit whining, Sergeant. You need to build up those…"

Hiss… The four young men halted as the pod clicked, and, with the hiss of escaping air, swung open. Inside was a small, blond-haired boy. The boy waved and said, "Hi guys, what's new?"

"Put it down!" ordered the lieutenant. Then he grabbed Scotty by the shirt and demanded, "Get up!"

"Going my way, fellows?" Scotty quipped.

"I've heard of a lot of rebel tricks, but smuggling children; that's a new one," said the lieutenant.

"I'm not a member of the rebellion," Scotty said.

"Then who are you?"

Scotty sighed, this was perhaps not the time for the whole truth, but it was time for the most important truth. He declared, "I am a servant of the Lord Jesus Christ who is coming to destroy you and free His people!"

The lieutenant sneered, and he looked like he wanted to hit Scotty, but he refrained. Instead, he said, "More rebel brainwashing. Take him to a holding cell. We'll deal with him later. Take the pod back to the bay and have it analyzed, and find the B.O.T. he was with! I'm going to go report all this to Emperor Chu.

~

"T-minus three hours and counting, Commander," reported Lt. Fields.

"Thank you, Lieutenant," then she turned to Smith, "Commander Smith, any word from *Command*?"

"Yes, Commander; Admiral Carter is coming with a back up of two ships. They will be here in less than two hours," she replied.

"Two ships? Let's hope it's enough."

"Unless they are resupplying, the SYCO ships usually give the Earth a wide berth. The closest one right now is out past Neptune."

"Hmm…we just destroyed one of their sister ships. You would think that would put them a little more on the alert. Regardless, we can't afford to let this mission fail on our account. Begin intense system checks. I want this ship to in tiptop shape before we even think about heading into combat again," commanded Brooks.

"A tall order for three hours, but we'll get it done, Commander."

~

Loso had spent the last few hours wandering the halls of the Space Port. He had heard no word about Scotty from the several conversations he had eavesdropped on, and he was growing restless. At one point, he had even returned to the docking bay, but the security crew was long since gone and Scotty apparently with them. In one last act of frustration, he shouted, "By the blood of my programmers, where is Scotty Fields?"

"The prisoner Isaiah Scott Fields II, of the rebellion, is in detention chamber seven," replied the station's onboard computer.

"Bingo!" thought Loso as he headed towards the detention center at a run.

In detention chamber seven, Scotty sat on the cold steel floor. As he hugged his legs closer to his beaten and battered face, he remembered the events of the last few hours. After a short walk through some meandering halls, and an even shorter elevator ride, the Nazis had brought him here. Soon thereafter, two Japanese soldiers had entered the room. Scotty had no idea who they were at first. One was probably in his early twenties and his uniform sleeves were rolled back. The second man was clearly much older, but not *old* by any means. He never said a word, but his eyes burned with the passion of the Devil. The younger man called him Emperor Chu, and Scotty had no doubt believing this man was capable of all the evil the rebels had told him about. Clearly God's plan of prophecy was being played out differently in this reality, but if this Earth was to have an Antichrist, Saki Chu certainly looked the part.

Throughout the interrogation, the younger officer had asked many questions, and each unsatisfactory answer had ended with a fist in Scotty's young face. His metal tipped boots had also been put to work, fracturing most of his ribs and bruising most of the rest of his body. It wasn't long before the young Emperor of Staranana had been reduced to a sobbing lard. He couldn't recall Seth, or even Lizard Face being this cruel to him (though Lizard Face had certainly tried), and it was usually moments like this when Joshua showed up; but the angel was nowhere in sight.

Finally Chu spoke, "I know you are not what you seem to be, boy. Your DNA matches that of a boy reported missing at the lunar colony last year."

"You mean you never had a chance to eject me into space?"

"Indeed, but I suspect that there is more to your story. Much more! My officers tell me that the pod you were concealed in has technology they have never even imagined, and the controls are written in a language they have never seen before. In fact, no one on Earth has ever seen the language before."

"They should read more!" Scotty mocked.

Chu nodded at the younger officer, and his fist went flying again. This one sent a tooth flying from Scotty's mouth – one of his last baby teeth he hoped, but he suspected that was wishful thinking.

Chu folded his arms behind his back and began to pace around the boy crumbled in the middle of his cell. He said, "I must say, boy, you take a beating much better than other boys your age – even better than some men."

"This isn't my first beating, and in my line of work, I suspect it won't be my last."

"Well, let's make sure this is one to remember."

The Nazi emperor began to roll up his own sleeves, but a voice from the intercom halted him, *"Emperor Chu, this is the station commander. There is something up here that I think you'll want to see. We have a fleet of rebel vessels converging on the station. They are holding position just outside our weapons range."*

"Understood, Commander. I'll be right there."

"Shall I continue the interrogation, Your Highness?" asked the younger officer.

"No, give him some time to think things over. If we can't get the answers we want, we'll do to him what was done to the rest of the lunar colonists." Then the two men left the detention area.

Scotty let out a desperate, exasperated breath, overwhelmed by a sense of failure and wincing at the pain in his ribs. Time was almost up for him to activate his pod, and from the Commander's report, the rebels were already moving into position. If they attacked before the magnetic field was activated, the Space Port would annihilate them. There had to be a way out of all this, but how?

These thoughts, and the throbbing pain in his head, were so overwhelming that he barely noticed the faint noise emanating all around him. However, as the noise grew steadily louder, it drew more and more of his attention. It was a clicking. No, wait, it was more of a buzz. "Now wait just a minute!" he thought. The sound had again changed. It had become a continuous chime. Standing, with much effort, he attempted to find the persistent sound. He pressed his ear against every wall and even the floor, but was unsuccessful. Eventually he did locate it just beyond the cell's door, outside in the corridor. His cell being a solid box with no windows, he still couldn't see what it was, but it was growing louder with every passing second.

Soon the sound was so loud that the very brains within his skull rattled. He backed away from the door, and with a bone shattering sonic boom, the reinforced steel door crumpled to the deck. A cloud of smoke rolled in and with it came a dark figure. The figure stepped into the light and spoke, "Begging your pardon, sir, but we have little time to spare. We must get moving!" Scotty was so thrilled to realize that the snaggle-toothed figure was Loso that he rushed from the room without a word.

"I managed to disable the security units in this area, but we have to hurry. We only have five minutes left," warned Loso already dashing down the corridor, or at least moving as quickly as his mechanical legs could carry him.

Scotty said nothing, and though the effort of running made him want to pass out from the pain with every step, he kept running. Soon they were sliding down elevator shafts and dashing through obscure corridors - both to avoid the Nazi and to make it to the docking bay in time. Loso's course worked, and they arrived with three minutes to spare. However, the complete Nazi security team that greeted them caused just a touch of further delay.

"Stop right there!" demanded a dragon-eyed man. Scotty recognized him as the tyrant Saki Chu.

"Sir, I was..." Loso muttered nervously.

"Be silent! Agent Loso!"

"How do you know who I am?" the B.O.T. dared to ask.

"We've known for some time that the rebels have a B.O.T. in their ranks. You see, you are not the only ones to send spies into your enemy's camps. However, today will be the end to that particular advantage on your part. My officers tell me they should be able to decipher the technology in your pod within a few weeks. Assuming it holds all the secrets we believe, we will..."

As Chu rambled on, Scotty moved a hand slowly to his belt and flipped a switch on a special panel located there. On the other side of the bay, his pod lit up and began to hum, and then a miracle happened. Saki Chu turned toward the noise, and his eyes widened as half-a-dozen energy bolts leapt from the pod and enveloped he and his men. They all collapsed to the deck, unconscious.

"Move it!" shouted Loso, as he climbed into his *TSJ*, and Scotty simultaneously climbed back into his pod. With no time for goodbyes, Scotty checked all his systems. They were fine. Once his scanners indicated that Loso was safely out of the station, he activated the magnetic field. And Spikey did not disappoint; in a flash of rainbow light, his pod was scooped up in the *Door* field, and he was gone.

~

"Admiral Carter's ships are ready, Commander," reported Eli calmly.

"Good, let's do it!" ordered Brooks.

In a single instant that sent Lt. Fields's heart leaping into his throat, he maneuvered the *Intruder* into the Space Port's weapons range. By that point, the Port should have been nothing more than a hulk of metal floating in space, but the *Intruder's* scanners, and those of her sister ships, revealed something far more terrifying. Every light of the Space Port was still illuminated, and a green pulse of tachyon energy was heading right toward them. The Nazis knew!

But something was wrong. The pulse seemed sluggish and was beginning to fizzle out of existence, and the station's lights were dimming. A few more seconds passed, and the entire station went black.

"Move in!" shouted Brooks in excitement, practically pole-vaulting down to the helm.

"Confirmed," complied the other ships. The battle, if one could call it that, was short. The rebels seized the Space Port in less than an hour. Something about the crippling of their station and every weapon onboard by a simple magnetic field took the heart out of the Nazis' fight.

It wasn't long before Smith was reporting, "I am detecting escape pods leaving the station, Commander. The defense barrier around the planet has collapsed, and they are heading for the surface."

"How can they operate their pods without computers?" Scott asked.

"The pods have some sort of manual propulsion systems installed," Eli reported.

"Shall I open fire, Commander?" Smith asked.

"No, let them go. We have more important things to do. We need to get the station and the defense net up and running again before any SYCO vessels start heading our way. Contact Admiral Carter, and ask him to have his boarding parties secure every major system. I can only imagine what kind of surprises the Nazis might have left behind."

"Admiral Carter is already waiting on the line for you, Commander."

"Open a channel," Brooks ordered, and she stiffened in her command chair as the holographic image of a graying, but no less commanding man formed on her bridge.

"Well done, Lori! Frankly, I expected the Nazis to put up a bit more of a fight."

"I don't suspect we've seen the last of them."

"Neither do I, which is why we need to move quickly. If we can reprogram the station's computers and reestablish the defense net, we can keep them bottled up for years. Intelligence reports only four Nazi vessels are currently on patrol in the solar system – no match for the station."

"Perhaps, not, but if the Nazis managed to get off a distress signal, or launch any of their ground ships, we should be anticipating trouble at any moment."

"Then let's get to work, Captain."

"Uh, I'm just a commander, sir."

"Not anymore. We can discuss the details of your promotion later, but I've no doubt you've earned it. And something tells me you'll be up to the challenge of your new post."

"New post?"

"Take a look out the window, Captain, and welcome home."

After

"Scotty, you can't!" Spikey Moonbeam shouted, and yanked *The Prism's Echo* from the boy's hands and snapped it shut.

Scotty's eyes glazed over for an instant, and he looked like he was going to pass out. He caught himself on the edge of the table and looked up into the face of the elder bear, "Spikey?"

"Yes?"

The boy looked around him. "What happened to my pod?"

"Pod? What pod?" Sparkey asked.

"I wasn't in an interdimensional travel pod?"

Both bears shook their heads.

"No…no, I was inside that book! Wow, Spikey you were right. I was not ready. I totally lost myself in there, though I did remember Staranana – just a different version of it where I got sucked into an alternate universe by one of your inventions."

"You barely opened the book before I yanked it out of your hands. How much time did you experience in there?"

"A few days I think."

"What did you see?" Sparkey asked.

"Myself."

"What?"

"In a manner of speaking anyway. The book created a reality where the Nazis did fall after World War II, but eventually they rose to power again and dominated not only the world, but the solar system as well. I was onboard a spaceship called the *Intruder*, which was part of the rebellion. Serving onboard that ship was a duplicate of me."

"The book didn't put you in the place of that character?" Spikey asked.

"No, we were totally separate. In fact, we didn't exactly get along very well. The rebels helped me get back here in one of your inventions that I guess does not even exist."

"Not yet anyway," Spikey smirked.

"And I helped them commandeer the Nazi Space Port. It was all incredibly real."

"Yes, and dangerous. I think we need to learn more about this book before any more of us try to use it," Spikey cautioned.

"You're right, and besides, it's not like Staranana isn't exciting enough as it is without having to resort to fantasy. Still…"

"What is it, Scotty?" Sparkey asked.

"Well, I can't help but wonder if there is more to *The Prism's Echo* than mere possibility. What if, somewhere out there beyond all we know, there is a reality where all the people I met really are struggling against a tyrannical Nazi regime, or all the people Spikey met are really struggling against an evil sorceress named Morgana le Fay.

Spikey thought about that for a moment and then said, "If that is the case, then I would say they all definitely need our prayers."

~

The Adventure Continues in Book 2...

Parallel Encounters: Salvage

Other exciting titles from *Thrive Christian Press* include:

Chronicles of the Imagination: Staranana
ISBN 978-0-9800600-1-0

After enduring centuries under a vicious tyrant, the people of the icy planet Staranana must decide whether to abandon their faith or continue to trust in the promises of God. The results of that decision will spark an adventure beyond the imagination!

Chronicles of the Imagination: Lizard Face
ISBN 978-0-9800600-3-4

A time of peace has dawned, but on the eve of the first Christmas on Staranana, an ancient enemy returns. Faith, friendship, and family will all be tested, and a single wrong decision could very well spell the doom of Staranana!

Chronicles of the Imagination: Nana-Old Testament
ISBN 978-0-9800600-6-5

The Staranananians find themselves stranded in Earth's biblical past, and if they are to find their way home, they'll have to enlist the help of some of the greatest characters from throughout the *Old Testament*.

Chronicles of the Imagination: Nana-New Testament
ISBN 978-0-9800600-7-2

Having been trapped in the biblical past for months, hope is fading from the hearts of the Staranananians. If they are to make it home, they must seek out the source of hope Himself, but this adventure won't end until the blood of one of them has been shed.

Find them today at www.amazon.com in paperback as well as on *Amazon Kindle* and *Barnes & Noble Nook*.

Check out these other *Classroom Classics* from *Thrive Christian Press*:

Rudyard Kipling's The *Jungle Book* – *Enhanced Classroom Edition*
ISBN – 978-0-615-70585-9

From Mowgli's relentless battle against the man-eating tiger Shere Khan to Rikki-Tikki-Tavi's great war against the sinister cobras Nag and Nagaina, Rudyard Kipling's classic *The Jungle Book* has been filling our lives with excitement for more than a century now. No personal library is complete without this timeless novel, and this edition enhanced for use in the classroom is a must have for any teacher about to embark on this literary adventure.

Steven Crane's *The Red Badge of Courage: Enhanced Classroom Edition*
ISBN – 978-0-615-80812-3

How does a coward become a hero? Henry Fleming is about to face that very question. Though he had, "...dreamed of battles all his life...", he soon finds that a soldier's life is more than he bargained for, and a single wrong decision runs the risk of branding him a coward for what little of his life he thinks he has left. Will he ultimately find the hero within, earning, if necessary, his own red badge of courage, or will he die a coward?

Sir Arthur Conan Doyle's *The Hound of the Baskervilles* –
Enhanced Classroom Edition
ISBN – 978-0-615-83170-1

There is a realm in which the most experienced of detectives is helpless – *The Supernatural,* and master detective Sherlock Holmes is about to plunge headfirst into that realm in this stunning adventure. *The Hound of the Baskervilles* takes Holmes and Dr. Watson to the Baskerville Estate where a mysterious hound of Hell has caused the deaths of many members of the Baskerville family. Will Holmes be able to crack this case before the latest heir to the Baskerville fortune meets his demise?

Also available…

To Kill a King
ISBN 978-0-9800600-8-9

Linna, a fighter in training in the
futuristic city-state of Domina, has
been marked for death by her own
father. Her only hope of survival is
to assassinate an enemy king, but is
she brutal enough to carry out the
deed?

Green Elephant – A "You Can Write" Activity Book
ISBN 978-1-4776-2830-0

Is there a great writer in you? *Green Elephant – A "You Can Write" Activity Book* uses a story written by a child to teach children how to write stories. The activity book also includes space for young authors to write their own stories and draw their own illustrations.

Thrive Christian Press is eager to see the Gospel of Jesus Christ spread throughout the world. If you would like 70% of the royalties from your most recent purchase donated to a Christian missionary or ministry of your choice, please complete the form below and mail to:

Missionary Donation Request
Thrive Christian Press
1120 Huffman Rd. Ste. 24-447
Anchorage, AK 99515

Missionary Name _____

Christian Ministry _____

Ministry Address _____

_____

Ministry Website _____

       Can we donate via this site?   *Yes*   *No*

Ministry Email _____

Title Purchased _____

Retailer Amazon.com   CreateSpace.com   Barnesandnoble.com

Please include a copy of your receipt. Visit www.thrivechristianpress.com to submit your request via email. Click on the *Mission Support* tab.

*All donations are subject to verification of the Christian ministry in question and purchase. Not all Thrive Christian Press titles qualify. Donations will be made in electronic form on ministry websites. Payment will be made within 60 days of request. This form is for paperback titles only. Please visit www.thrivechristianpress.com to request a donation for a Nook or Kindle title.

Donations by Title & Retailer

The Betrayal of Kelcott

Amazon	CreateSpace	B&N	Kindle	Nook
$1.00	$1.85	$0.17	$1.46	$1.36

Chronicles of the Imagination: Staranana

Amazon	CreateSpace	B&N	Kindle	Nook
$1.47	$3.16	N/A	$1.95	$1.81

Chronicles of the Imagination: Lizard Face

Amazon	CreateSpace	B&N	Kindle	Nook
$1.37	$3.05	N/A	$1.95	$1.81

Chronicles of the Imagination: Nana-Old Testament

Amazon	CreateSpace	B&N	Kindle	Nook
$0.83	$2.93	N/A	$2.44	$2.27

Chronicles of the Imagination: Nana-New Testament

Amazon	CreateSpace	B&N	Kindle	Nook
$1.00	$3.00	N/A	$2.44	$2.27

Green Elephant

Amazon	CreateSpace	B&N	Kindle	Nook
$1.67	$3.00	$0.24	N/A	N/A

The Hound of the Baskervilles

Amazon	CreateSpace	B&N	Kindle	Nook
$1.50	$2.90	$0.09	$1.96	$1.68

Parallel Encounters

Amazon	CreateSpace	B&N	Kindle	Nook
$1.00	$1.85	$0.17	N/A	N/A

All donation amounts are subject to change at any time and without notice. Donations are made to legitimate Christian organizations only, and all such organizations should be in close agreement with the Thrive Christian Press statement of faith. Requests for donations to organizations that do not meet these criteria will be declined. Purchase required to donate, but purchase does not guarantee donation. See www.thrivechristianpress.com for more details.

www.ingramcontent.com/pod-product-compliance
Lightning Source LLC
Chambersburg PA
CBHW020640130626
46552CB00003B/1320